W9-BZT-096

WITHDRAWN

WITHDRAWN

GOODNIGHT LAB

A Scientific Parody

Copyright © 2017 by Chris Ferrie
Cover and internal design © 2017 by Sourcebooks, Inc.
Cover design by Sourcebooks
Cover and internal illustrations © Chris Ferrie

Sourcebooks and the colophon are registered trademarks of Sourcebooks, Inc.

All rights reserved. No part of this book may be reproduced in any form or by any electronic or mechanical means including information storage and retrieval systems—except in the case of brief quotations embodied in critical articles or reviews—without permission in writing from its publisher, Sourcebooks, Inc.

The characters and events portrayed in this book are fictitious and are used fictitiously. Any similarity to real persons, living or dead, is purely coincidental and not intended by the author.

This book is a parody and has not been prepared, approved, or authorized by the creators of Goodnight Moon or their heirs or representatives.

Published by Sourcebooks, Inc.
P.O. Box 4410, Naperville, Illinois 60567-4410
(630) 961-3900
Fax: (630) 961-2168
sourcebooks.com

Library of Congress Cataloguing-in-Publication Data is on file with the publisher.

Source of Production: Qualibre, Shenzhen, Guangdong Province, China
Date of Production: September 2017
Run Number: 5010345

Printed and bound in China.
QL 10 9 8 7 6 5 4 3

GOODNIGHT LAB

LAB

A Scientific Parody
by Chris Ferrie

sourcebooks
jabberwocky

In the great green lab,
There was a laser
And a lab notebook
And a picture of—

"Imagination is more important than knowledge."

Albert Einstein

Einstein with a stern look

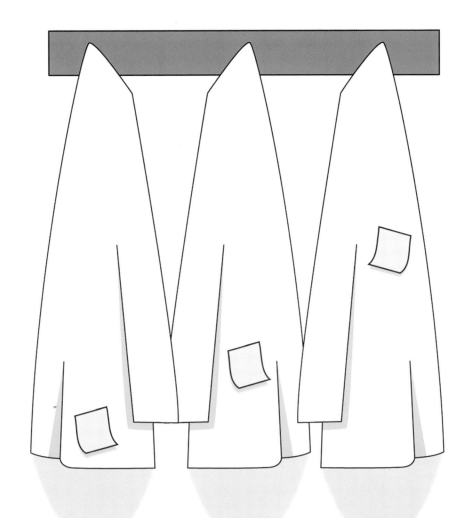

**And there were three sticky notes
stuck to lab coats**

And copper wire
And a pair of pliers

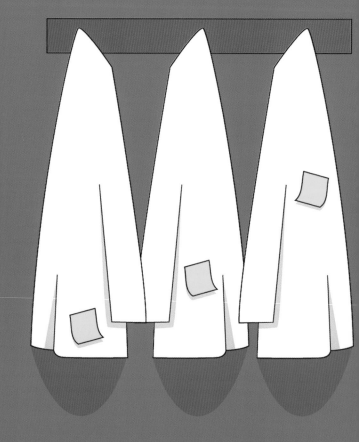

And a spectrometer
And a thermometer

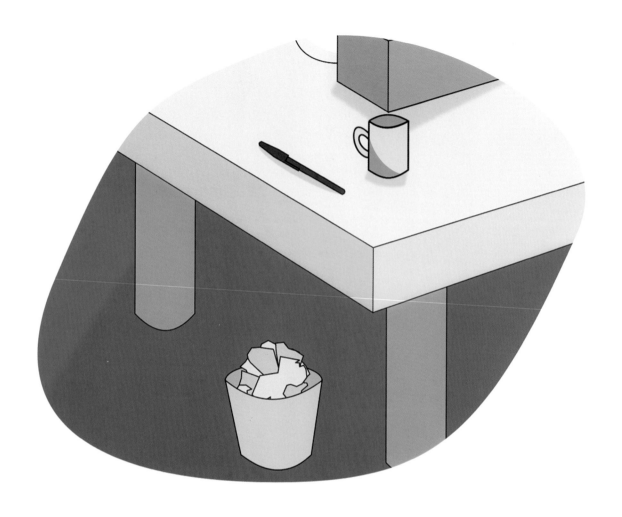

**And a pen and a coffee
And some crumpled rubbish**

**And a grumpy old professor
shouting "publish"**

Goodnight lab

Goodnight laser

"Imagination is more important than knowledge."

Albert Einstein

Goodnight Einstein with a stern look

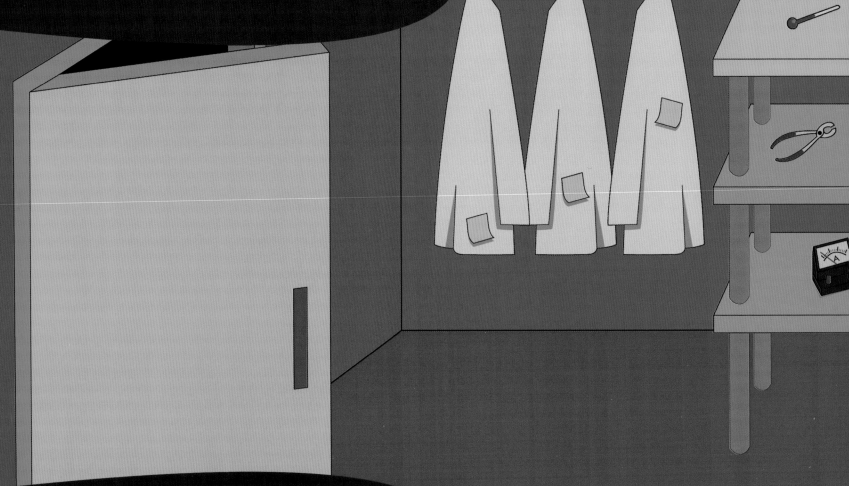

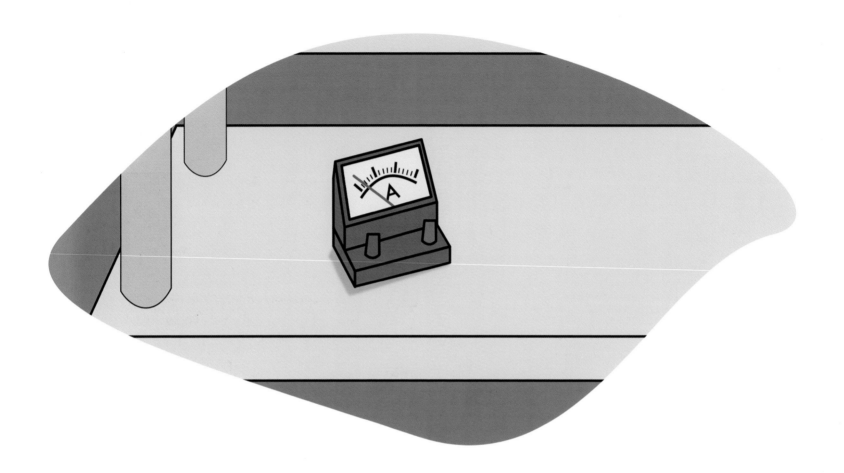

Goodnight ammeter

And goodnight voltmeter

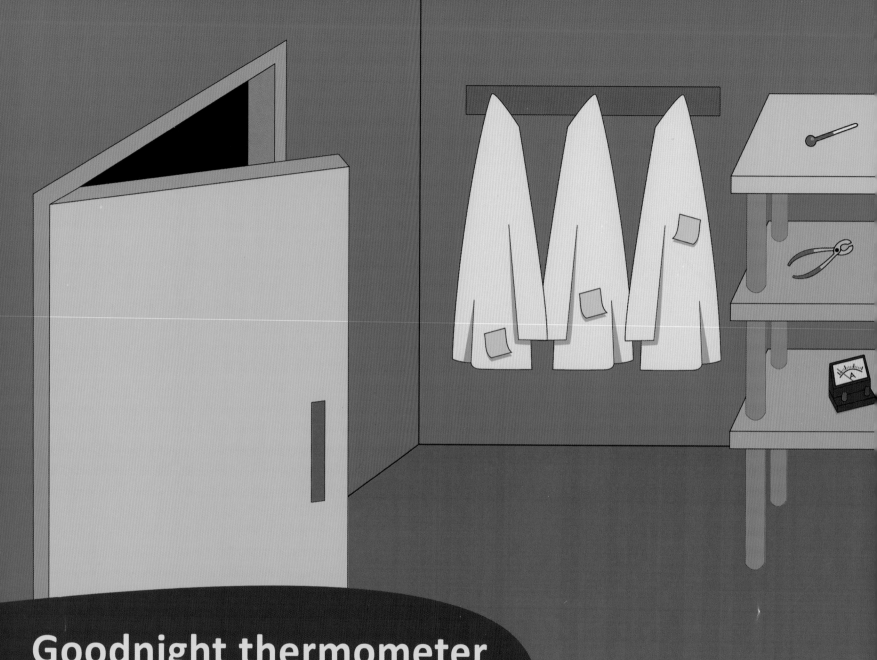

Goodnight thermometer
Goodnight spectrometer

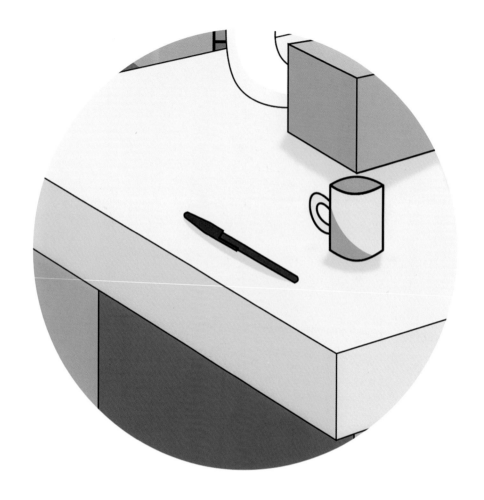

Goodnight pen

And goodnight rubbish

Goodnight to the grumpy old professor shouting "publish"

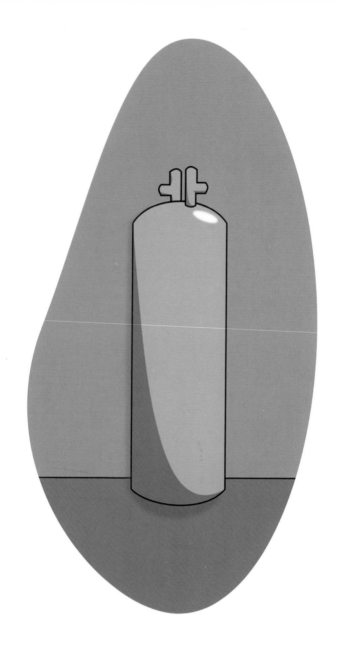

Goodnight liquid nitrogen

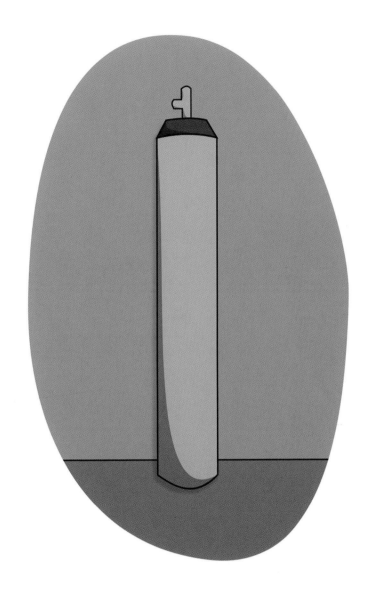

Goodnight compressed air

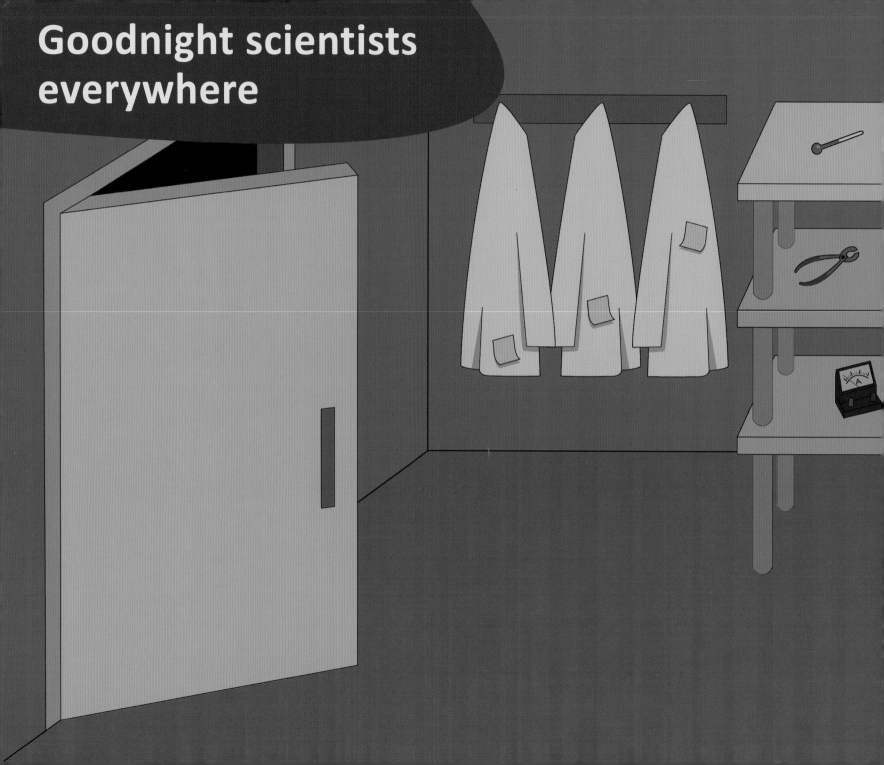

Goodnight scientists everywhere

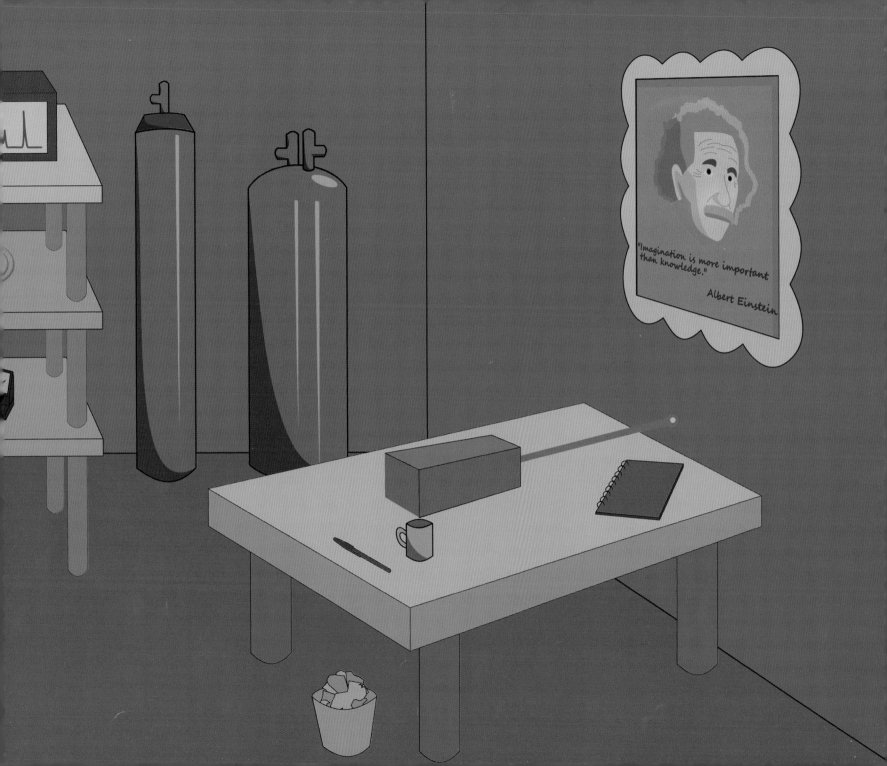

"Imagination is more important than knowledge."

Albert Einstein

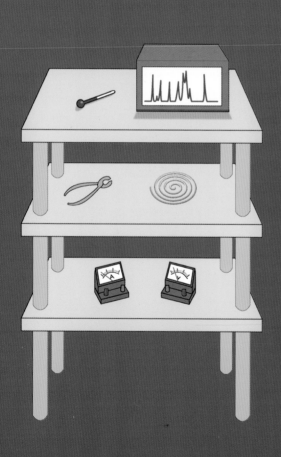

"Imagination is more important than knowledge."

Albert Einstein

Chris Ferrie is a physicist, mathematician, and father of four budding young scientists. He believes it is never too early to introduce small children to big ideas!

Learn more from Chris Ferrie's Baby University series

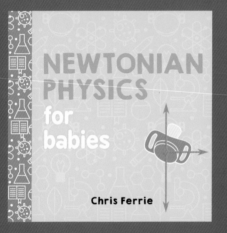

NEWTONIAN PHYSICS for babies

Chris Ferrie

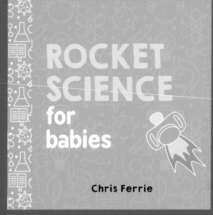

ROCKET SCIENCE for babies

Chris Ferrie

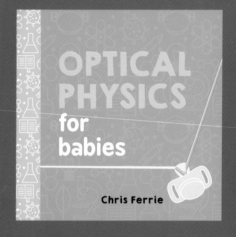

OPTICAL PHYSICS for babies

Chris Ferrie

GENERAL RELATIVITY for babies

Chris Ferrie

QUANTUM PHYSICS for babies

Chris Ferrie

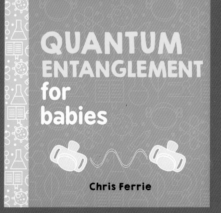

QUANTUM ENTANGLEMENT for babies

Chris Ferrie